This Is the NEST That ROBIN Built

with a little help from her friends

For my good friend
Wendy Watson

BEACH LANE BOOKS
An imprint of Simon & Schuster Children's Publishing Division
1230 Avenue of the Americas, New York, New York 10020
Copyright © 2018 by Denise Fleming
All rights reserved, including the right of reproduction in whole or in part in any form.
BEACH LANE BOOKS is a trademark of Simon & Schuster, Inc.
For information about special discounts for bulk purchases, please contact
Simon & Schuster Special Sales at 1-866-506-1949 or business@simonandschuster.com.

CIP data for this book is available
from the Library of Congress.
ISBN 978-1-4814-3083-8 (hardcover)
ISBN 978-1-4814-3084-5 (eBook)

The Simon & Schuster Speakers Bureau can
bring authors to your live event.
For more information or to book an event,
contact the Simon & Schuster Speakers Bureau
at 1-866-248-3049 or visit our website at www.simonspeakers.com.
Book design by Denise Fleming and David Powers
The text for this book is set in Futuramano.
Manufactured in China
1217 SCP
First Edition
2   4   6   8   10   9   7   5   3   1

The illustrations were created using print-making techniques combined with collage.
Visit DeniseFleming.com for crafts and activities.

DENISE FLEMING

This Is the NEST
That ROBIN Built

with a little help from her friends

BEACH LANE BOOKS • New York   London   Toronto   Sydney   New Delhi

This is the SQUIRREL
who trimmed the twigs, not too big,
that anchor the nest that Robin built.

This is the DOG
who brought the string, long and strong,
that wraps round the twigs, not too big,
that anchor the nest that Robin built.

This is the HORSE
who shared his straw, rough and tough,
that covers the string, long and strong,
that wraps round the twigs, not too big,
that anchor the nest that Robin built.

This is the PIG
who mixed the mud, soft not soupy,
that plasters the straw, rough and tough,
that covers the string, long and strong,

that wraps round the twigs, not too big,
that anchor the nest that Robin built.

This is the MOUSE

who gathered the weeds, dotted with seeds,
that bind the mud, soft not soupy,
that plasters the straw, rough and tough,
that covers the string, long and strong,
that wraps round the twigs, not too big,
that anchor the nest that Robin built.

This is the RABBIT
who picked the grass, fresh and sweet,
that cushions the weeds, dotted with seeds,
that bind the mud, soft not soupy,

that plasters the straw, rough and tough,
that covers the string, long and strong,
that wraps round the twigs, not too big,
that anchor the nest that Robin built.

These are the EGGS,
brittle and blue,
that lay on the grass, fresh and sweet,
that cushions the weeds, dotted with seeds,
that bind the mud, soft not soupy,
that plasters the straw, rough and tough,
that covers the string, long and strong,
that wraps round the twigs, not too big,
that anchor the nest that Robin built.

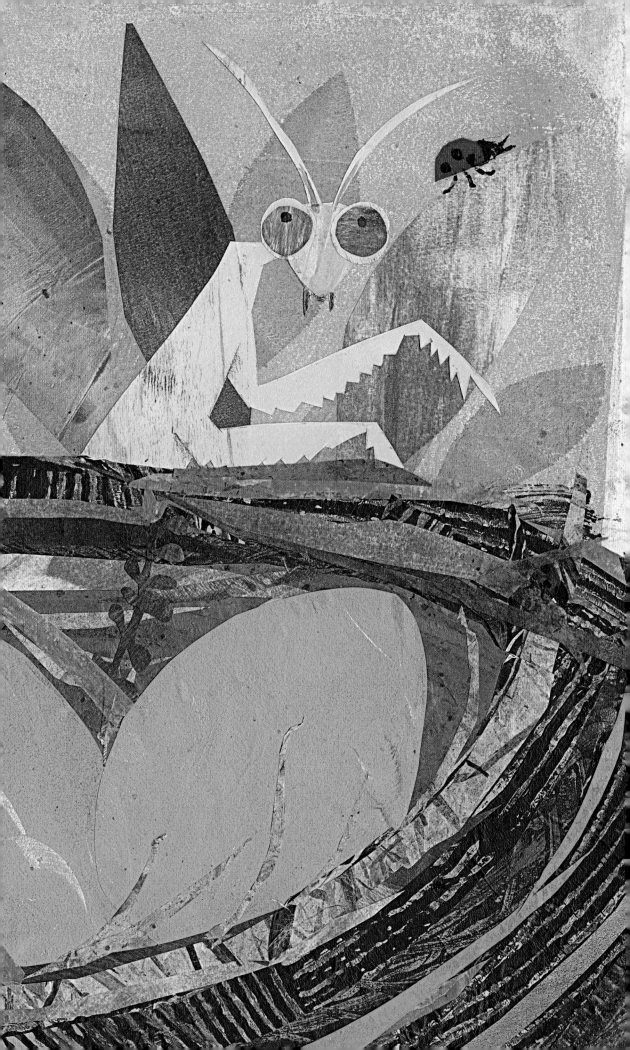

These are the NESTLINGS,
tufted and pink,
that cracked the eggs, brittle and blue,
that lay on the grass, fresh and sweet,
that cushions the weeds, dotted with seeds,

that bind the mud, soft not soupy,
that plasters the straw, rough and tough,
that covers the string, long and strong,
that wraps round the twigs, not too big,
that anchor the nest that Robin built.

And this is the ROBIN
who built the nest . . .

wrapped with string,
long and strong,

covered with straw,
rough and tough,

cushioned with grass, fresh and sweet;

cracked by nestlings, tufted and pink . . .

anchored with twigs, not too big,

plastered with mud,
soft not soupy,

bound with weeds,
dotted with seeds,

who laid the eggs, brittle and blue,

now young FLEDGLINGS,
rumpled and ruffled, and ready to fly.

Good—

bye!